GOSCINNY AND UDERZO
PRESENT
AN ASTERIX ADVENTURE

ASTERIX AND THE MAGIC CARPET

WRITTEN AND ILLUSTRATED BY UDERZO
TRANSLATED BY ANTHEA BELL AND DEREK HOCKRIDGE

HODDER AND STOUGHTON

LONDON   SYDNEY   AUCKLAND

Asterix and the Magic Carpet

British Library Cataloguing in Publication Data

A catalogue record for this book is available from the British Library

ISBN 0 340 40957 6 (cased)
ISBN 0 340 42720 5 (limp)

Original edition © Les Editions Albert René, Goscinny-Uderzo, 1987
English translation © Les Editions Albert René, Goscinny-Uderzo, 1988
Exclusive licensee: Hodder and Stoughton Ltd
Translators: Anthea Bell and Derek Hockridge

First published in Great Britain 1988 (cased)

First published in Great Britain 1989 (limp)
This impression 120 119 118 117 116 115 114 113

Published by Hodder Children's Books
a division of Hodder Headline plc
338 Euston Road, London NW1 3BH

Printed in Belgium by Proost International Book Production

* The power to make people laugh: from an epigram by Caesar on Terence, the Latin poet.

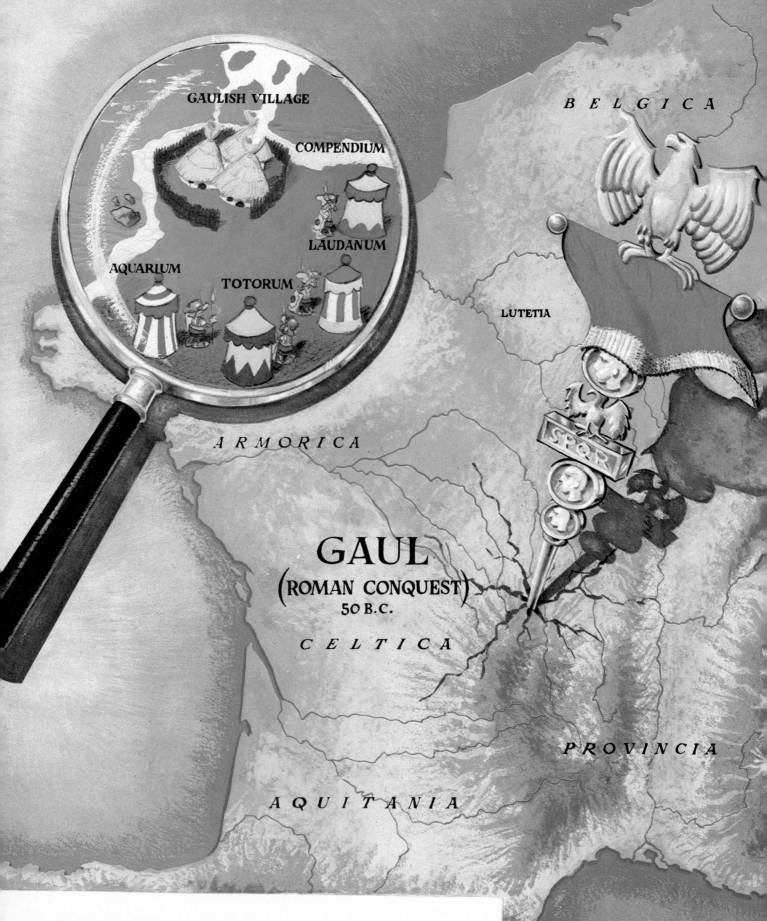

GAULISH VILLAGE

COMPENDIUM

LAUDANUM

AQUARIUM

TOTORUM

ARMORICA

BELGICA

LUTETIA

GAUL
(ROMAN CONQUEST)
50 B.C.

CELTICA

PROVINCIA

AQUITANIA

The year is 50 BC. Gaul is entirely occupied by the Romans. Well, not entirely... One small village of indomitable Gauls still holds out against the invaders. And life is not easy for the Roman legionaries who garrison the fortified camps of Totorum, Aquarium, Laudanum and Compendium...

6

8

9

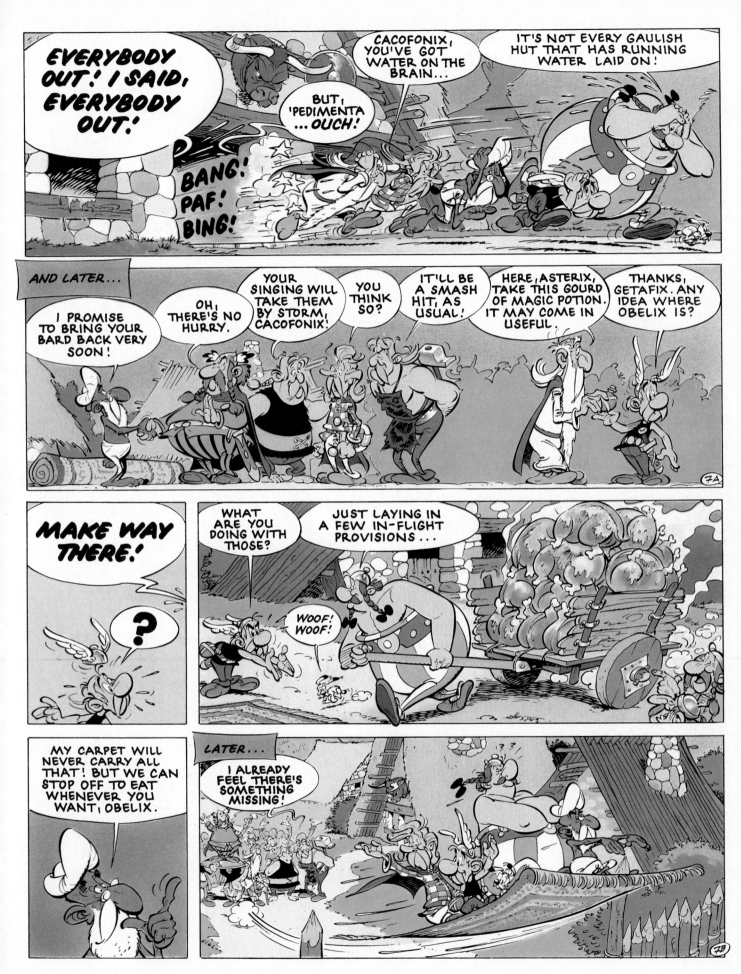

11

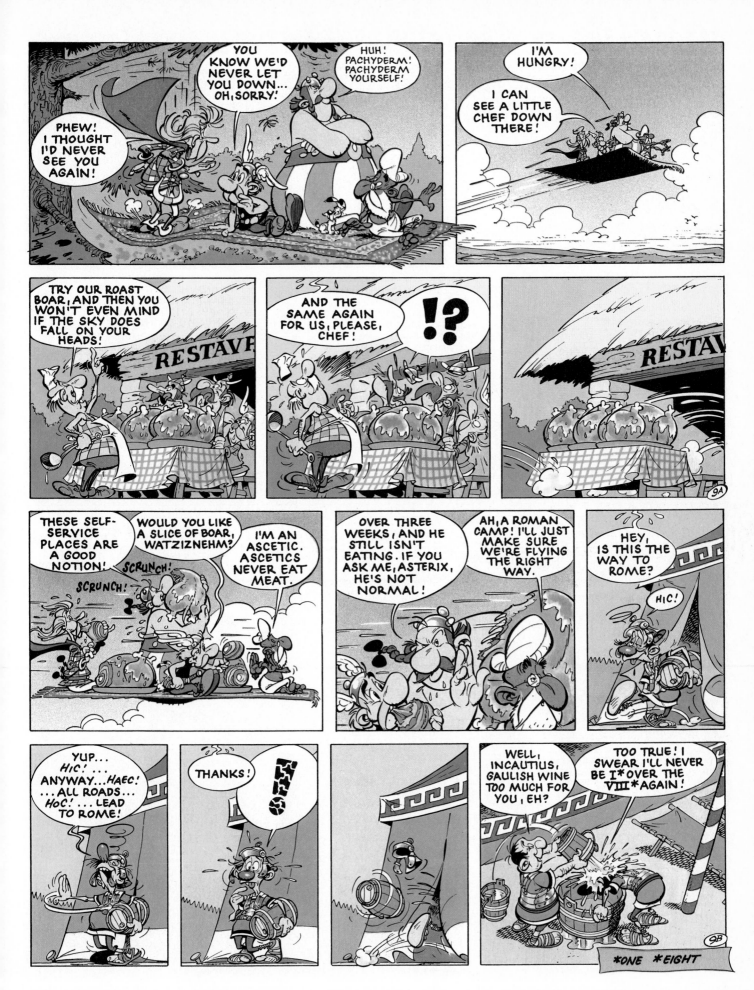

13

15

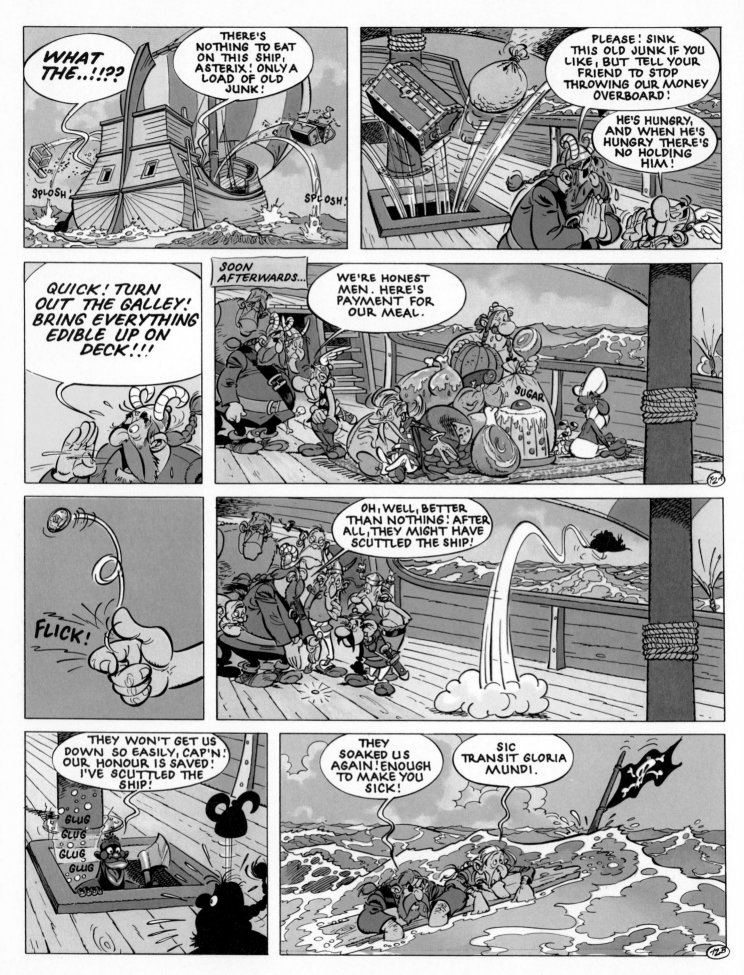

17

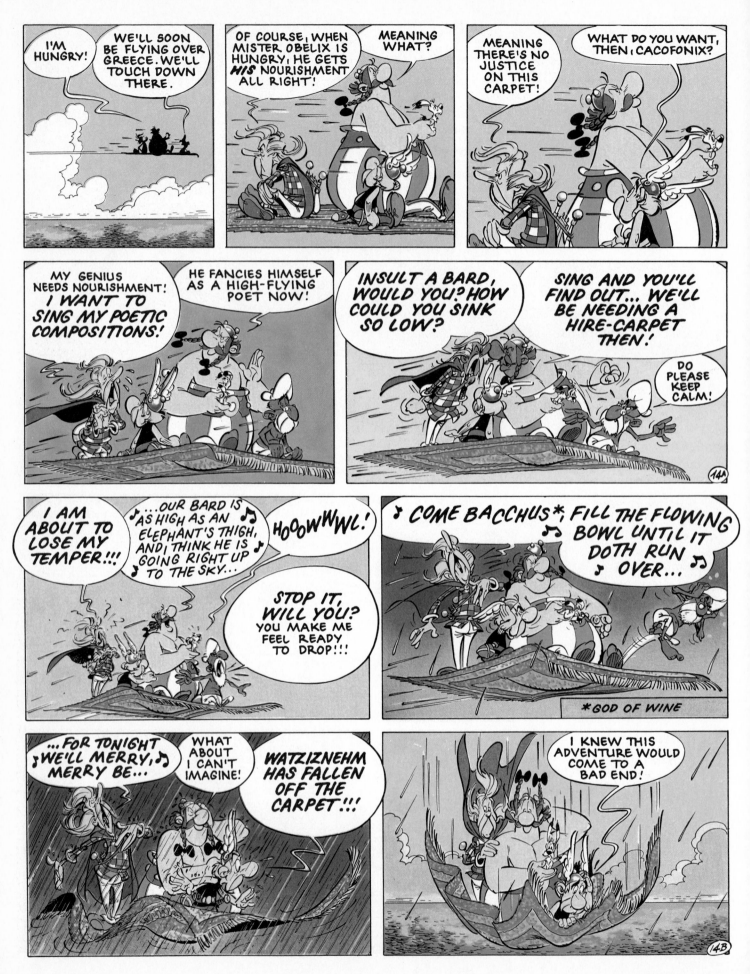

18

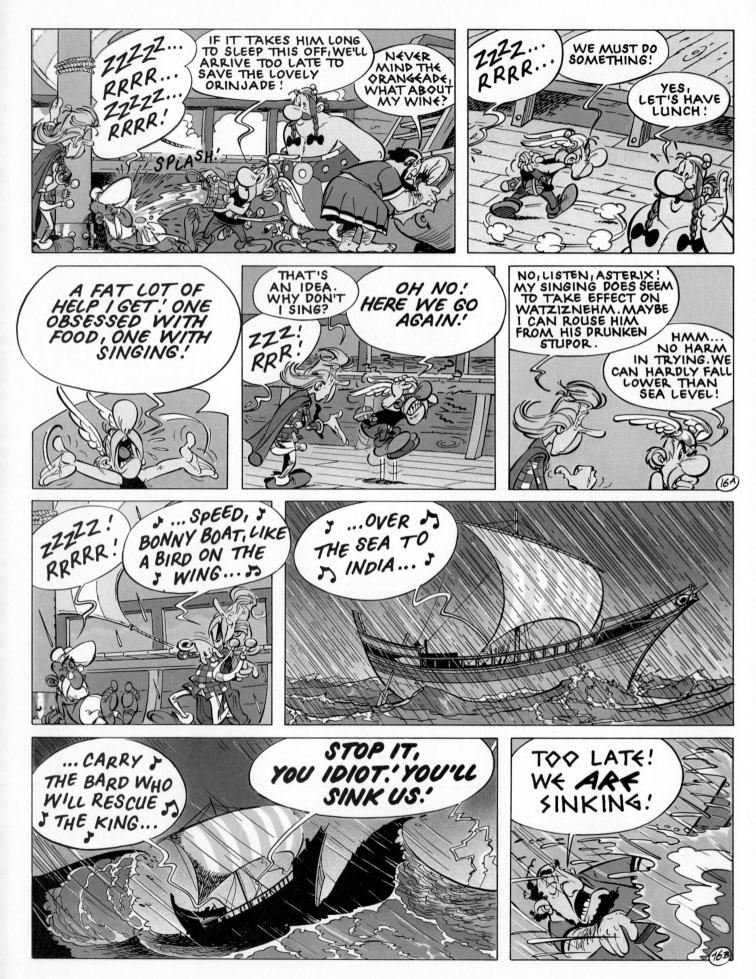

20

21

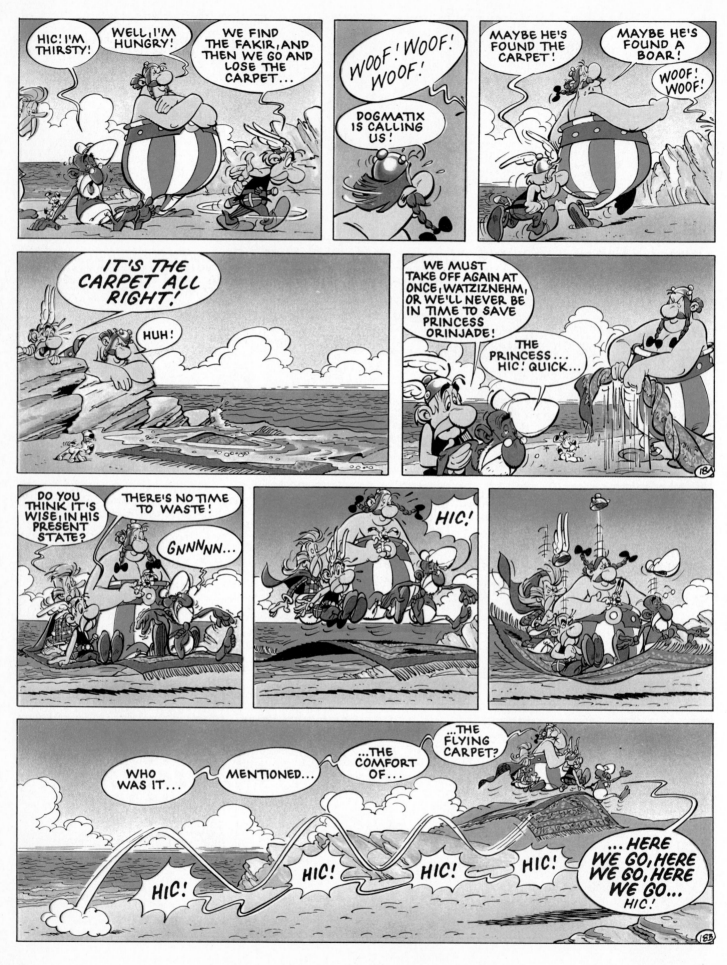

22

23

26

27

28

A ROAST CAMEL MAY BE A GOOD BUY, BUT IT'S NOT UP TO A GOOD ROAST BOAR!

NO ONE WOULD EVER KNOW, SEEING THE AMOUNT YOU ATE!

RIGHT... NOW WE'VE FILLED UP AGAIN, WE MUST MAKE UP FOR LOST TIME AND FLY STRAIGHT TO RAJAH WATZIT'S KINGDOM!

I WILL NOT SEE YOU DIE, DEAR ORINJADE! I'D RATHER ABDICATE IN FAVOUR OF HOODUNNIT.

DON'T WORRY, FATHER! WATZIZNEHM ISN'T JUST ANYONE!

NO KNIGHTS IN SHINING ARMOUR RIDING TO WATZIT'S AID AS THE THOUSAND AND ONE HOURS TICK BY, OWZAT!

NO, IT WOULD TAKE A THOUSAND AND ONE NIGHTS TO SAVE HIM AND THE PRINCESS NOW!

O HOODUNNIT, DIVINE MASTER, SUPPOSE THERE'S STILL NO RAIN WHEN YOU'VE EXECUTED THE PRINCESS?

INDRA WILL CALL FOR MORE ROYAL BLOOD... AND IT'LL BE OFF WITH THE RAJAH'S HEAD!

BUT SUPPOSE IT *STILL* DOESN'T RAIN?

IT WON'T MATTER A BIT, BECAUSE BY THEN I'LL BE RAJAH MYSELF. HO, HO, HO!

HOWEVER, THE VALIANT PERSIAN CARPET FLIES TIRELESSLY ON, WHETHER CROSSING BAKING DESERTS...

...OR FACING THE BITTER WEATHER OF THE MOUNTAIN PEAKS.

AS SCENERY GOES, THIS LEAVES ME COLD!

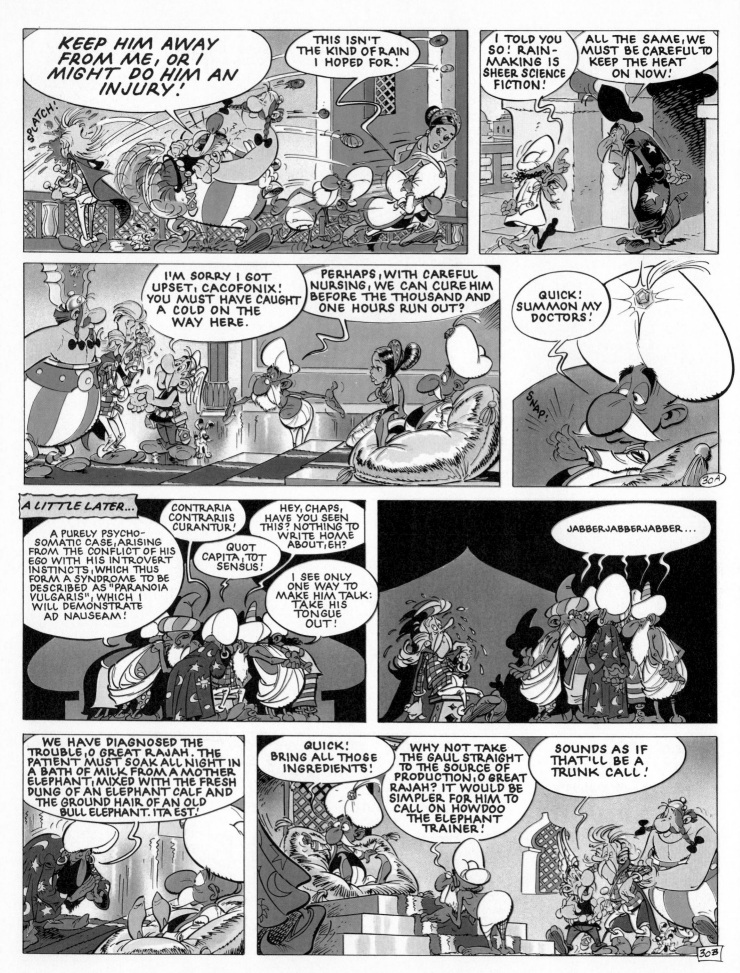

34

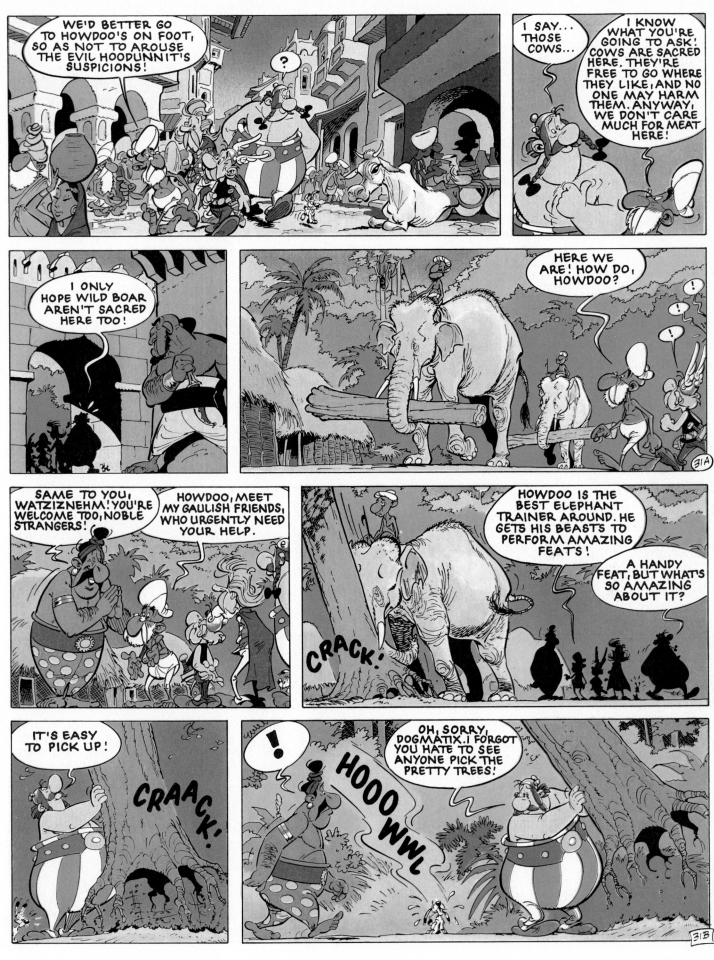

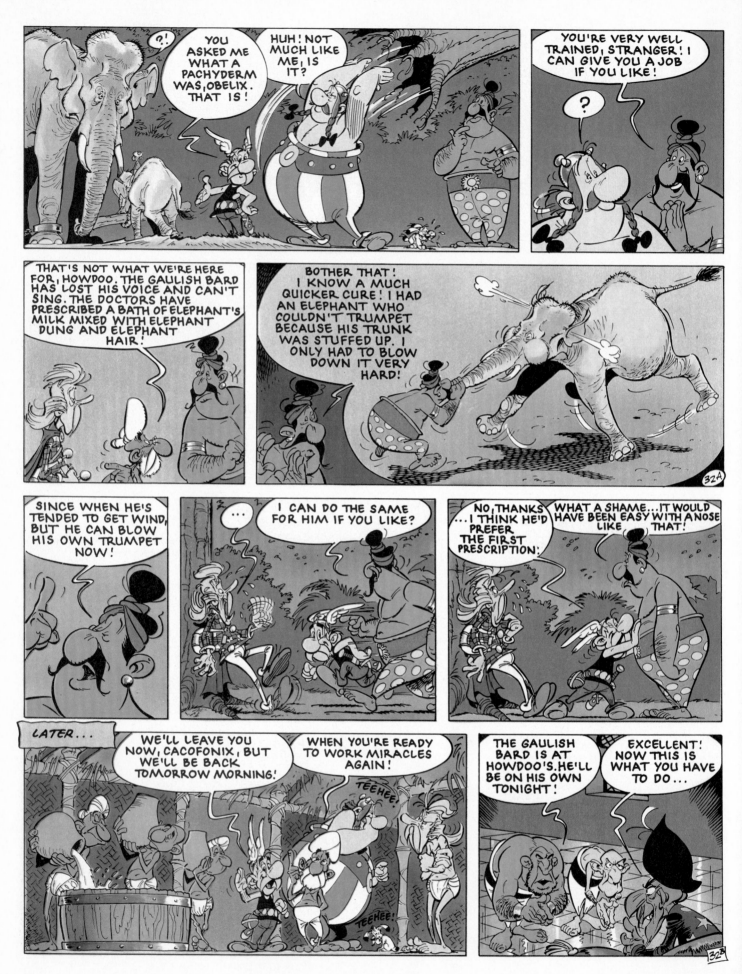

36

38

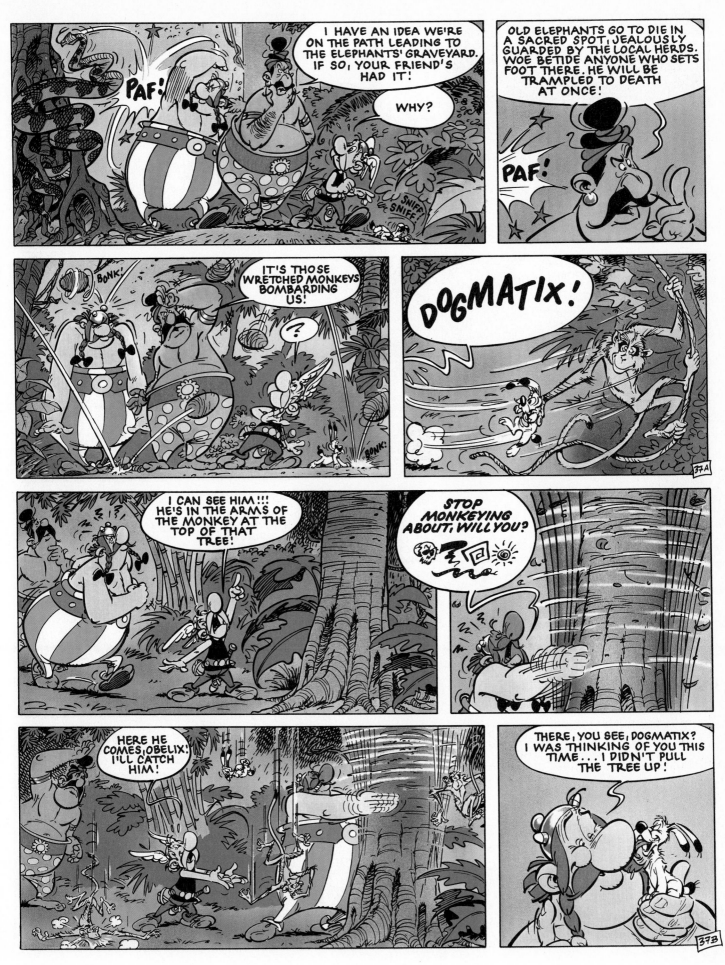

42

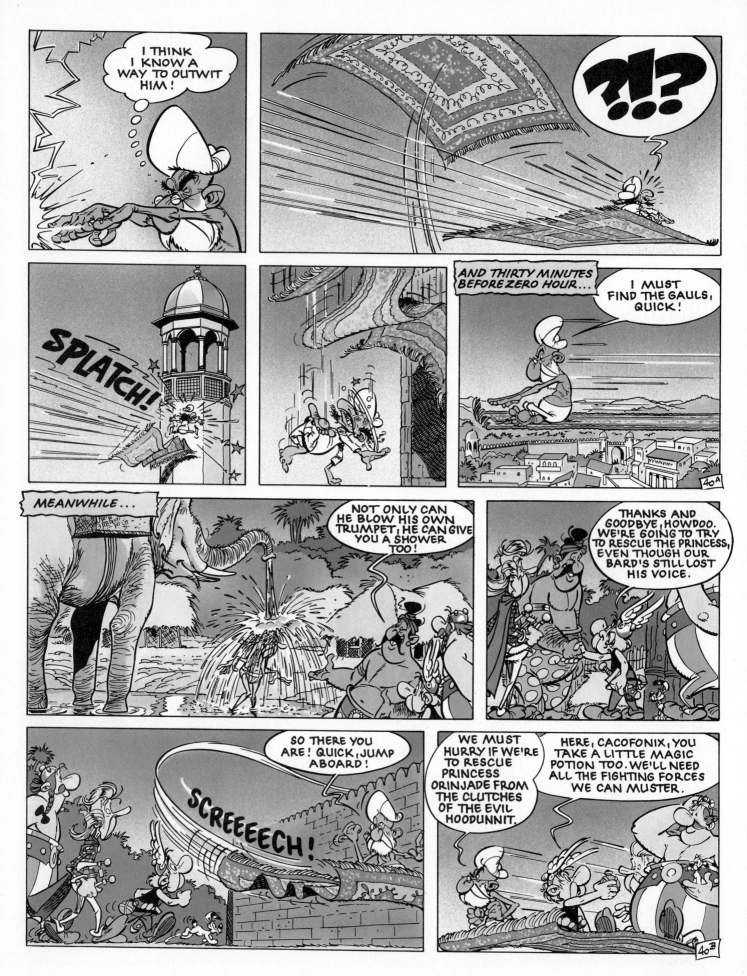

46

THE END

—UDERZO—6·8·7

48